Glasgow Dreamer

Glasgow Dreamer

IVOR CUTLER,
drawings by MARTIN HONEYSETT

METHUEN

First published in the United Kingdom by
Methuen London 1990

This edition published in the United Kingdom in 1998
by Methuen Publishing Limited
20 Vauxhall Bridge Road, London SW1V 2SA

Random House Australia (Pty) Limited
20 Alfred Street, Milsons Point, Sydney,
New South Wales 2061, Australia
Random House New Zealand Limited
18 Poland Road, Glenfield,
Auckland 10, New Zealand
Random House South Africa (Pty) Limited
Endulini, 5A Jubilee Road, Parktown 2193,
South Africa

1 3 5 7 9 10 8 6 4 2

Text copyright © Ivor Cutler 1990, 1998
Illustrations © Martin Honeysett 1990, 1998

Ivor Cutler has asserted his right under the Copyright,
Designs and Patents Act, 1988, to be identified as the
author of this work.

Methuen Publishing Limited Reg. No. 3543167

A CIP catalogue record for this book is available from
the British Library

ISBN 0 413 73600 8

Printed and bound in Great Britain by
Butler & Tanner Ltd, Frome and London

To vowels,
the lubrication that stops consonants
from sticking together like boiled sweeties
in a paper bag*

* example in Czech of what happens if you don't use them:
strč prstskrz krk. (Trans: *Stick the finger through the neck.*)

Glasgow Dreamer

Episode One

Glasgow Glasgow, where are you?
Forty four from Edinburgh.

'Cover the melon with your cap,' whispered Father,
as the heads of our relations appeared at the top of the
stairs, nostrils twitching, lips in a loose wet smile,
throbbing salivary glands, moved to the table and
draped their soft buttocks over our worn chairs.
We stood and watched.

'Ivor,' said Father in a quiet tone, 'fetch some leaves off
the tree.'

I took a large white plate off the shelf and slipped
downstairs. As I reached and tugged off the big juicy
leaves, my body trembled with pleasure. Father was
taking a stand.

I returned with a full plate and 'Annie Laurie' on my
tongue.

'Here you are, folks!' said Father, taking the plate and
slapping it down before them. The smiles faded.

'I've never been so insulted!' screamed Auntie Rose.

'Let's get out of here!' rasped Uncle Sam, 'you've not
heard the last of this.'

They rose and stamped down the stairs, slamming the front door. I stood at the window to see them off. Father embraced me.

'Come on, Ivor' he chuckled, and we ate up the melon, then went off to see Rangers v. Celtic and chew Wrigley's P.K.

Mother's white face greeted us on our return. She said nothing, but when I went to bed – oh boy!

Glasgow Glasgow, where are you?
Eighty four from Stranraer.

Episode Two

Glasgow Glasgow, where are you?
Ninety three from Oban.

'Come on, Ivor,' called Grandfather, and we set off for
Queen's Park Pond, he with his walking stick, me with
my fishing net and jam jar.

We scuttered across Pollokshaws road like insects,
avoiding tramcars with mixed success. 'Bishopbriggs
via Springburn' – 'Rouken Glen via Giffnock'. These
were faraway places, like India and China, though the
passengers carried no luggage and looked just like
pedestrians sitting down.

Once inside the safety of the park, we made our way
to the pond, Grandfather to a bench, and me to the
bagaminnies, a close relation of the English minnow.

They were not in a hurry to be caught, like the peas and
barley in Scotch broth, so my scoops became wilder and
eventually the cane slipped from my hand. In a panic,
my heart on my tongue, I ran to the bench.

'Can I borrow your walking-stick, Grandfather? I've
lost my fishing rod.' Away in another place, another
time, he nodded.

'Be careful. Don't lose it.'

I dashed back with it and reached out. The rod was slippery and cheerily avoided the stick. I held the point and tried to hook it with the handle, but it just went further out and smiled.

In despair, I threw the walking stick at it. They just lay there in the water, two bits of stupid wood, obeying the laws of nature. I stood and watched them, waiting for a breeze to spring up and drift them to the shore. In vain.

I turned to face Grandfather's wrath. Then we sat and waited.

Glasgow Glasgow, where are you?
One five one from Mallaig.

Episode Three

Glasgow Glasgow, where are you?
One eight five from Fraserburgh.

'Where are we going, Father?' I muttered, gazing at my
sandals.

'It's Hypocrisy Day,' he replied. 'Stop looking at your
sandals and come on.'

We ran to the great square. Father melted into the
background and I joined a queue of little hypocrites.
When I reached the counter I was handed a piece of
charcoal and a clay figure with a wooden head.

I pondered, then drew my brother's face on the sanded
wood, returned the charcoal and joined a queue at a
gibbet in a quiet dusty corner. I waved at Father with my
free hand, but he was lying across a heap of broken
yellow bricks, studying the greyhound page.

My turn soon came. I hanged my brother and stood
back, crocodile tears filling my eyes, then let him down,
and, on a theatrical childish impulse, popped my head
into the noose and hanged myself.

There was a hush, then Father swaggered over and let me down, just as my face was turning from red to blue, and clouted my head several times to restore my natural pallor.

The disappointed crowd heaved a great sigh. We joined them, to soak in the holiday atmosphere. There was a brisk east wind and we could smell the fecund Edinburgh middens, forty miles distant.

Glasgow Glasgow, where are you?
Twenty six from Dunoon.

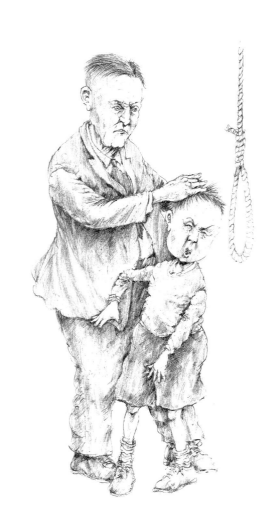

Episode Four

Glasgow Glasgow, where are you?
One four two from Aberdeen.

I was given a Lexicon for my birthday. To be out the way,
I went into the bedroom and emptied the cards on to the
carpet. Then I sat and looked. The intense black and
white – I could make any word I wanted – I could make
UP words.

My brain swam and I felt a little sick with power.
Reaching forward I wrote 'Ivor', then 'Cutler'. It was
my first bit of publicity. After that, I lost interest.
It was the power to make the words that excited me,
not the making.

I stuffed the cards back in the box and stuck it into my
pocket. I felt like a giant. Then I strode back to the
kitchen and we sat round the table and played. It was a
poor sort of game, without any magic; something you
did with your head, like crosswords.

Last year, I came across a Collins pocket crossword dictionary in the secondhand part of a bookshop. And there they all were – words and words and words. My eyes darted about the pages. Wherever I looked – words.

Dizzy, I snapped shut the book. It was like a brand new cabinetmaker's toolbox. I wondered whether I, alone, deserved such a book – such a private pleasure, so I hurried through to the new section and bought six more copies, which I presented with reverence to poets and people like that.

But I still feel guilty. Perhaps you're not supposed to look at words all naked, but wait till they're in sentences, and decent. One day I shall come to terms with my private pleasures and become less furtive.

Glasgow Glasgow, where are you?
Fifty two from Kirkcaldy.

Episode Five

Glasgow Glasgow, where are you?
Fifty one from Crianlarich.

My big brother came rushing home from school,
bursting from his first biology lesson – and I was to
hand.

'He taught us about babies.'

'Mhm,' I breathed, my head in a comic.

'How do you think the world keeps on going if
everything didn't keep on multiplying and reproducing?'

'Everything?' I murmured, to keep the pot boiling, as I
was just about finished.

'Yes. People and plants and animals. There's male and
female. Then they mate and the female has the baby.
That's how the world keeps going.'

I sat up. I was finished. 'How do they mate?'

'Oh, I don't know yet. Mr Espie'll probably tell us
next week.'

'Is that how there's stones?' I'm not interested in
moving things.

'I expect so. You just get a female and a male and they
mate and then you get another stone.'

I stood up and ran down to the back green for a couple
of stones. I found a bit of smooth red brick for the
female and a big cinder in the midden for the male and
brought them upstairs. You grow bulbs in the dark, so I
fastened an elastic band round the stones to keep them
together, placed them on the top shelf at the back of the
hall press and shut the door.

Every day after school I had a feel at them. Finally I
spoke to my brother. He looked at them.

'I think they're both female. That's why it's not
working.' I stared at him. Then took them downstairs
and threw them against the washhouse till they broke.

Glasgow Glasgow, where are you?
Sixty one from Perth.

Episode Six

Glasgow Glasgow, where are you?
One three four from Campbeltown.

When I was three I caught a disease and was sent to stay with my father's parents, who lived at Abbotsford Place in the Gorbals.

That was a great treat, because I got sleeping in the kitchen bed and could smell the kitchen table, scrubbed with blue and white marbled soap. There was a black sink with a brass swan-neck spigot which swung forward and down.

I sat on the wooden draining-board and played with it, watching the trains cross the bridge, dispersing thick black clouds over the Gorbals.

'Get away from the water!' shouted Grandmother perfunctorily.

One morning, Grandfather entered the kitchen clad in his woollen combinations. I jumped down from the bed and walked towards him. My head was on a level with his groin, from which a collection of unknown fleshy objects protruded.

I extended my puny finger and sank it into his fluted scrotum. 'Is this your gizzard, Grandfather?' I piped.

He chuckled and shuffled back to the bedroom.

'He he he he he!' cackled Grandmother, on receipt of the news.

What had I said? I can still remember the warm sound of their pleasure.

Glasgow Glasgow, where are you?
Twenty five from Lanark.

Episode Seven

Glasgow Glasgow, where are you?
One seven two from Kyle of Lochalsh.

We walked to Maxwell Park Pond. Father had heard that
the pond was frozen. Our white breath bumped against
our faces, and if you breathed into your scarf it got wet.

By the time the park railings showed up, dusk was
falling. We ran onto the ice.

I wonder how deep the water is? A useful space was
found between the ice and the edge and, like a two-and-
a-half-year-old scientist, I lowered my left leg in to see
how far it would disappear.

But I had not reckoned the degree of concern which my
right leg would show. Bereft, it followed the left to see
where it had gone, and in a few seconds, hardly worth
the counting, I was happily ensconced below the ice,
looking peacefully through it at the dark grey sky –
a magic moment.

Alas, I was grasped roughly, like a fish, and hauled
ashore.

Then, having ascertained that I was alive and therefore still worth their concern, I was carried at full speed to a distant relation nearby and given a hot bath and chocolates out of a big tin.

Actually, I drowned, and moved on to the next universe to continue my existence, leaving my body behind, a tiny frozen corpse, to the crocodile tears of my nearest and dearest.

That's what really happens when you die.

Glasgow Glasgow, where are you?
One one one from Braemar.

Episode Eight

Glasgow Glasgow, where are you?
One O one from Berwick-upon-Tweed.

When I was six we moved from Ibrox to Shawlands.
As the wooden ladder was missing, I volunteered to
accompany Father in retrieving it.

On the way back, the conductor would not let us on to
his tramcar, so we walked along, me at the back, Father
snapping at my speed.

The local school was Shawlands Academy, and I was
put into Miss Whyte's, top infants, and anonymity.
The desks were swingtops.

One afternoon I noticed that Donald Macdonald had
his desk up and was rubbing snot up and down on it.
This revolted me: it was like masturbating, a function
I had yet to discover in public. My open hand rose.

'Yes, Ivor?' croaked Miss Whyte, who had white hair in
both senses and would soon retire.

'Please Miss Whyte, Donald Macdonald's picking his nose and rubbing it up and down the desk.'

'Donald Macdonald, you dirty boy. Stop that at once. Thank you, Ivor.'

I looked round for the glances of scorn that would surely be directed at Donald. Instead the whole class were looking at me with hatred. I shrank, bewildered.

A late developer, I had yet to realise that others had worlds of their own. A hopeless egocentric, I would only be fit to go on the stage when I grew up, which was the only direction available to me in those days.

Glasgow Glasgow, where are you?
Seventy four from Dumfries.

Episode Nine

Glasgow Glasgow, where are you?
One five one from Grantown-on-Spey.

One Sunday, after dinner, I was told to stay in. At three
o'clock the bell rang and a tall man was taken into the
big room. I sat in the kitchen and quaked.

'Ivor!' called Father. I jumped, in time with my stomach,
my heart, my nervous system, then dragged my feet into
the big room to dree my weird.

'This is my son Ivor,' said Father to the stranger.
The man turned a look of such patent honesty and
goodness upon me that I was appalled and affronted.
How dare he set up such unfollowable standards? He was
God, disguised as a cubmaster touting for recruits.
There was no escape.

A fortnight later, clad in a green cap with yellow piping,
a scratchy navy jersey and a neckerchief held by a braided
leather woggle, I entered a stuffy hall packed with my
peers.

An unsavoury smell, sweet and sickening, hit my neb. I never traced its source. Perhaps it was the smell of disorientated little boys warming up new, unwashed uniforms with their body heat.

We performed a lot of character-forming rubbish perfunctorily, then returned home.

It was a weekly battle to get me to go, the cost of the uniform being brought up. Finally I won, and was left in peace until my father started a troop of scouts.

When I was seventeen, I saw a headline in the *Daily Record* and joined the Royal Air Force Volunteer Reserve. My character is still unformed, thank goodness. That smell!

Glasgow Glasgow, where are you?
Thirty three from Ayr.

Episode Ten

Glasgow Glasgow, where are you?
One seven nine from Elgin.

My big brother is a great
story-teller. His best story is
the one he told us when I
was four.

His teacher had a peesher
fifty yards long and was
obliged to wrap it round his
waist. One day, on his way
home from school, he
tripped, fell down a stank in
the sewers, and was covered
in cack and peesh.

That's the story.

He managed to spin it out
to maybe half-a-minute,
plus screams of laughter.
We made him repeat it
several times till our mother
came in and told us to shut
up and go to sleep.

Today, his stories have
become more sophisticated.
He is too wise to try to
repeat his early success.

Glasgow Glasgow, where are you?
Seventy six from St Andrews.

Episode Eleven

Glasgow Glasgow, where are you?
Sixty nine from Galashiels.

I belonged to three gangs before I discovered girls. The
first had six members, each with a notebook and pencil.
We elected a president, a secretary and a treasurer. The
other three wanted office, so they became vice-
president, chairman and, though we only had a hazy
notion of what it meant, a convenor. Then we fought and
the society broke up.

The Black Triangle Gang followed. We met in Queen's
Park at a ring of boulders and jumped with indifferent
skill from boulder to boulder.

The last gang was called Gli Horyo. Horyo was short
for Hook oryon oheeoh, the first line of a Gaelic song
taught us by Marie S. Irving, the school music teacher.
To distinguish us, Peter spelled his gli, LLI, and Alex,
LYI. I got the GLI as I'd thought it up.

Peter was the extrovert, given to singing songs right in
your face. Alex and I were introverts and a bit wary of
one another. He learned Gaelic and became a Scottish
Nationalist.

Peter and I went for walks along the River Cart, discussing Marilyn Monroe's sponge and smoking Black Cat to the background of a delightful odour, which I didn't smell again till 1960, when I traced it to the wife of Johnny Mortimer, ace trombonist. She called it Diorama, which Christian Dior have discontinued, bad cess to them. The smell, in the wild, is wild garlic, which I couldn't have known then, as people only used pepper and salt to cook with in those days.

Glasgow Glasgow, where are you?
Two eight five from Thurso.

Episode Twelve

Glasgow Glasgow, where are you?
Two one six from Ullapool.

When I was in the top juniors a pile of cards was dished
out – two apiece – for us to sign. On one we promised
never to smoke, on the other never to drink.

They were distributed by a Christian organisation.
I was a Jew, but that was no excuse, even though I took a
sip of prayer-quality wine every Friday night as we
welcomed in the Sabbath. I added my John Hancock to
the cards and passed them back, shades of prison
playing about in my head like old sooty cobwebs.

To the irritation of the family, I started preaching on the
evils of drink and tobacco. After all, twelve is a well-
known time for moral hypocrisy. I suppose it's the age
when children decide to become policemen and nurses
and teachers.

One day, at dinner – mince balls, potatoes and pineapple
chunks – Father, exasperated beyond bearing, burst out,
'Where do you get all this rubbish from?'

Excited, full of zeal, I pulled a pamphlet we had been given from my inside jacket pocket and flourished it. Unfortunately I rather spoiled the effect by inadvertently dislodging a packet of Black Cat, which skited along the tablecloth and fetched up against the tomato sauce, to hushed astonishment. Ivor the Good! Black Cat cigarettes!

I rose. 'Sit down and finish your dinner,' barked Father, 'and put these back.'

'I don't want them,' I choked.

'Take them,' he said, 'and finish them.' I slipped them back in my pocket and ate up, pondering Father's humanity. How could he know that the aesthetics of cigarettes had nothing to do with abstinence, and that hypocrisy was not in question?

Glasgow Glasgow, where are you?
Seventy six from Dundee.

Episode Thirteen

Glasgow Glasgow, where are you?
Eighty four from Pitlochry.

One morning, Mother fastened a fresh nappy on to me, pulled a pair of blue rubber pants over it and sat me in the cot. The rubber smell was new and exciting.

My hands sought out the hemless edge. To my delight, the rubber tore, soft and quiet. A deep satisfied peace entered me.

I sought out new areas to tear and, after a short space, the pants were in ribbons and I was a very happy boy.

When Mother came in to see me, she gave a cry of amused exasperation, fetched a second pair and fastened them on, removing the tatters.

'Oh, thank you,' I thought and went to work. The performance was repeated, minus Mother's amusement.

The third pair was torn in a perfunctory way. Sensual saturation having been reached, my heart was no longer in it, like an executioner having chopped off his hundredth head.

Mother entered the room, froze, her face bright red, and began to shout at me. It was my first crit. I was not being understood. I shall die not being understood, like the rest of you.

Glasgow Glasgow, where are you?
Two one seven from Dornoch.

Episode Fourteen

Glasgow Glasgow, where are you?
Eighty two from Lochgilphead.

When no one was home, Mother would fasten on my roller skates and I would push her round the flat, she balancing herself with the sweeping brush.

I learned a lot about her body as I grew taller. She had soft calves, muscular thighs and a corset. By the time my hands were level with the top of her corset, the fun had palled and we stopped by tacit agreement.

Initially, it was very difficult to get any momentum – she was a fleshy woman – so she'd bend over and undo the straps, I'd push the skates, she'd jump back on and fasten the straps while the skates were in motion – goodness knows how she kept her balance – and we'd set off down the hall, into the big room, round the table and back out, down to the kitchen, round the table and so on, till I was sweating, and Mother collapsed into a chair or on to the floor in hysterics.

She'd have put the kettle on before we started, so that a cup of tea was soon ready with a home-made biscuit.

You can imagine my astonishment, when, as a young man, I went dancing, and my right hand discovered that the corset was not a universal garment, and that women's flesh was not like custard, to be bound in else it would all fall out.

Glasgow Glasgow, where are you?
One O three from Fort William.

Episode Fifteen

Glasgow Glasgow, where are you?
One six nine from Inverness.

'Come on down to the midden,' called Emma Walker.
You did what Emma Walker asked. And anyway, she was
three years older. Her mother dressed in black, fed
beggars a slice of bread and a bowl of tomato soup,
which they ate on the stairs.

I went through the dunnie to the back green. There,
waiting for me, was Emma, and an ex of mine, Millie
Hamilton.

'Take your cock out!' whispered Emma, fiercely.

I undid my buttons and took it out, where it stood
blinking in the unaccustomed light. Millie produced a
dod of filthy cotton wool and fell to dabbing at it
purposelessly.

'That's enough,' said Emma in undirected disgust, just
as I was beginning to respond, and the pair of them
walked quickly away, without a thank you, leaving me
totally bewildered and a bit disappointed.

I suppose I was one of the props in some secret game.
And the cotton wool looked as if it had come off a sore
that was healing. I could have caught a disease and died
for all they cared.

I never played with them again, and exercised greater
initiative in future games with girls, in a dreamy way.

Glasgow Glasgow, where are you?
Twenty seven from Stirling.

Episode Sixteen

Glasgow Glasgow, where are you?
Seven miles from Milngavie.

Although Father's parents were desperately poor,
I vastly preferred their flat to my mother's parents'.
Each object, there being fewer, had a stronger identity,
and there were more matt surfaces.

Where there was a polished surface it looked ridiculous,
as it would in an old house in Rotterdam or Oslo. Matt
surfaces lie open and so allow the wood to communicate
its feelings.

When I entered the flat, wooden objects sniffed me like
an animal, then bade me welcome in their own way and
passed on the latest news, so limpid it became my
model.

On one occasion Grandfather downed a pint of sour
milk straight out the bottle, while Grandmother ate beef
fat dowsed in H.P. Perhaps out of embarrassment, she
praised their health-giving qualities.

It never occurred to me to ask Father why he didn't give them some money. I knew that we were always short, Mother running up big bills at the butcher and grocer, her first priority being her children's nourishment.

There's a seventeenth-century room at the London Museum where I go to sit and soak in the atmosphere of genteel melancholy. It's the nearest thing to being back with my grandparents, sharing the matt wood.

Glasgow Glasgow, where are you?
Seven miles from Milngavie.

Episode Seventeen

Glasgow Glasgow, where are you?
Only nine from East Kilbride.

The whistle blew at the end of play. I lined up facing the annexe, an attractive grey building made of weathered planks, within which sound carried like mad.

The teachers' lavatory was right by the entrance – a piece of sound Scottish architectural pragmatism; somebody knew the price of lead pipe.

Standing in the silent sunshine, a violent clanking burst out followed by Niagara as the cistern emptied. The door opened, to make sure the whole world could hear, and a beautiful student-teacher emerged in a silken dress, her golden hair glinting in the spring light.

A dapper athletic man-teacher in a well-cut dark suit appeared from nowhere and tried to enter the vacated room, but found his passage blocked. They smiled at one another, manoeuvred past, she to the classroom and he into the lavatory.

I stood there in shock. How could they have contrived to meet in such an unfortunate situation? How could they have smiled, each understanding the reason for their meeting, and in such fine clothes, and so good-looking?

Why did they not look embarrassed and ashamed, and avoid one another's eye, in a natural and seemly way? If you were that good-looking, did you have a superior kind of mores that allowed you to brazen it out?

I still cannot understand. AND in front of three whole class-loads of Scottish children.

Glasgow Glasgow, where are you?
One two seven from Kingussie.

Episode Eighteen

Glasgow Glasgow, where are you?
Fifty eight from Inverary.

It is nine o'clock. I am fifteen and I am going to kill myself.

My brother brought home a free sample of aspirin. Six tablets. Maximum dose, two tablets. I have appropriated them. Why am I about to take them? Because I have just realised that the world is a horrible place.

A 'Goodbye Everybody!' is left by the bed, I swallow the whole six with soft Glasgow water and set off for limbo.

To my irritated puzzlement, I awake refreshed at my usual time and rise to yet another day. What went wrong? I took three times the maximum dose.

I take the problem to my brother. He is a medical
student. It never occurs to me that he will pass the
information along. That he is unable, at eighteen, to
cope with what seems to me a simple question.

My mother and father are clearly embarrassed,
so, until I too am eighteen they treat me with kid gloves.
To my credit, I do not take advantage of their concern,
but just continue on my blind preordained dream.

Glasgow Glasgow, where are you?
One seven seven from Nairn.

Episode Nineteen

Glasgow Glasgow, where are you?
One three nine from Aviemore.

Mother was crouched at the kitchen table when I
returned from school. Her silence was portentous.

'Hello, Mammy,' I choked, to break the log-jam. She
swivelled and thrust a flimsy sheet of tired old paper
at me.

'Did you write this?'

My cheeks burned. It was a poetic love-letter. 'Yes,' I
whispered, humiliated by the invasion of my privacy.

'Why don't you take better care of your stuff?' She was
bitter. 'I was so affronted. What kind of reputation do
you think you're getting us? One of the neighbours
knocked on the door and said "I expect this belongs to
one of your sons. I found it on the stairs".' She paused.
'Just to give me a red face. Here! Take it out of my sight,
you bleggidge!'

I thrust it guiltily into my inside pocket and slunk off
into the bedroom, where I pulled it out. It was worse
than I feared. A practice letter, where I let go. 'Your soft
white breasts…'. I thrilled to my daring.

My auntie had a novel by James Barke where a man observes the delicate see-saw of a girl's hips as she crosses a bridge over a stream with a basket. Adult literature!

She caught me, and hid the book. I was less welcome at her house, my furtive adolescent eye an irritant, for she was a good-looking woman, and could do rather better than bake in *my* sweaty gaze. I've kept a lot of love-letters. They're awful rubbish.

Glasgow Glasgow, where are you?
Twenty one from Kilmarnock.

Episode Twenty

Glasgow Glasgow, where are you?
Seventy four from Ecclefechan.

Uncle Joe erupted into my life in 1927, with tobacco sets
for each of us, containing chocolate cigarettes,
chocolate cigars, chocolate pipes, chocolate matches,
chocolate-coated coconut pipe tobacco and a minute tin
ashtray fluted at the edge.

He had completed his contract with the regular army in
India as a signaller. He knew words like chubberol and
chorapeechy. His warm, rugged, handsome face was
irresistible, as were his tales, atrocious lies every one.
Our simple, spellbound faces were just as irresistible to
a man with a gift like his.

After a spell of doing nothing, he became a linesman,
fastening electric cables to the top of telephone poles.

One day he handed a silver sixpence to my big brother
for him to share out. We were four – three ha'pence
each. This became a weekly ritual till he married, when
it abruptly ceased. We were hurt, and my sister made a
point of asking for her arrears whenever they met.

One day when I was twelve, out in the car with my father and Uncle Joe in Renfrewshire, we passed a great stretch of land with enormous excavators and deep holes full of water.

'What's that, Uncle Joe?' He was the practical one.

'They're digging a new sea,' he replied.

'Wow! A new sea!' I thought, my imagination adrift, grateful for his succinct pragmatism.

Recalling the event when I was twenty-five, my cheeks went red with anger. What a cruel habit to tease children! And I resolved never to tease anyone for the rest of my life.

Glasgow Glasgow, where are you?
Eighty miles from Beeswing.